This igloo book belongs to:

....

igloobooks

Published in 2019
by Igloo Books Ltd
Cottage Farm
Sywell
NN6 0BJ
www.igloobooks.com

1019 002.01
2 4 6 8 10 9 7 5 3
ISBN 978-1-78905-195-7

Illustrated by Ian Cunliffe

Designed by Jason Shortland

Printed and manufactured in China

IAN CUNLIFFE

Megaboy

igloobooks

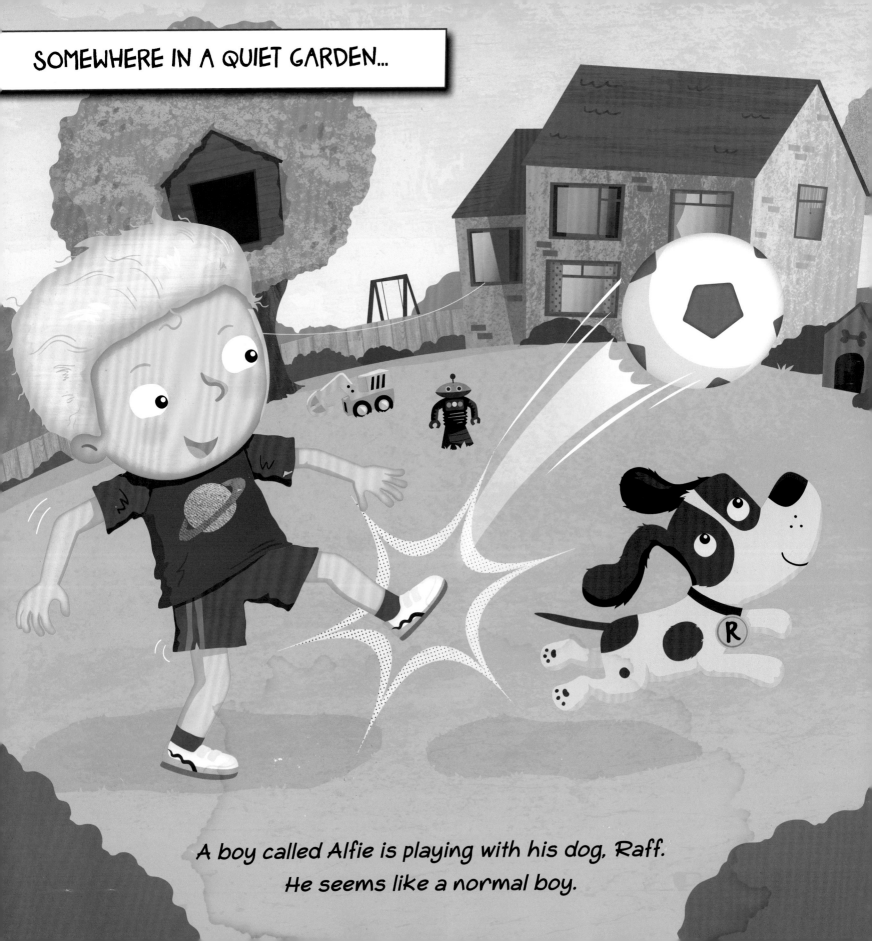

SOMEWHERE IN A QUIET GARDEN...

A boy called Alfie is playing with his dog, Raff.
He seems like a normal boy.

Alfie goes to school with his friends.

He argues with his big sister.

However, Alfie has a **secret.**
When no one is looking,
he transforms into...

The superheroes study maps, draw plans and watch over the town. There's just one thing standing in their way...

Dastardly Dad marches the scruffy pair to the
bathroom and plops them in the soapy water.

LATER THAT DAY...

Superheroes need super-food, so Megaboy mixes up a **super-powered** bowl of spaghetti, sweets and ice cream.

Megaboy and Megadog whizz towards the front door, ready to save the town again. Dastardly Dad stops them and orders them to clean their room.

Megaboy trudges up the stairs, grumbling.

The pair zip-line down
to the tree house.

Suddenly, the back door swings open...

Dastardly Dad helps
Megaboy and Megadog
climb down the ladder.
He's saved them!

"It's time for bed,"
says Dastardly Dad.
"I'll bring you both a big
mug of hot chocolate
to warm you up."

Megaboy and Megadog decide that Dastardly Dad isn't so bad after all. Dastardly Dad tucks the pair up in bed and reads them a bedtime story.

From now on, the superhero trio decide that,
instead of battling each other, they would work together
to keep the town, or sometimes each other, safe!